They all went out and played 'til bedtime!
"That was fun!" said Wolfie afterward.
"Come again soon!" said Little Bear.

Father Bear slowly
unlocked the door.
"Who's there?" he boomed. . .

Just then, **KNOCK KNOCK!** went the door. The house . . . went . . . very . . . very . . . quiet.

Father Bear came in from the yard.
"Goodness," he gasped. "What are
all your friends doing here?"

"They've
escaped from
a terrible wolf,"
said Little Bear.

So Little Bear sat them all down and started to read his story. But he kept being interrupted by a **Knock! Knock!** at the door.

First there was Little Red Riding Hood,

then Cinderella,

and finally Goldilocks.

They had all come to hide from the wicked wolf. "Don't worry," Little Bear told them. "You are all safe here."

"We ran for our lives," chorused the
sheep. "But he chased us!"
"We could hear him panting."
"We could feel his hot, wolfie breath."
"He was huge," baaed the sheep.
"He was fierce and angry," piped
the pigs.
"He was lean and mean," bleated Billy.
"And we didn't stop 'til we got to your
door," finished Bo Peep.

"Down in the field," panted Bo Peep. "I heard the hedge rustle, and I saw his bushy tail. And he bellowed . . ."

. . . Little Bo Peep and all
her sheep!
"Lock the door," cried Bo Peep.
"A wolf is after us!"
"What happened?" asked
Little Bear, as he quickly locked
the door.

KNOCK KNOCK! went the door!
"Who's there?" called Little Bear.
"It's Bo," said a voice.
"Please let me in."

Little Bear lifted
the latch, opened
the door and
in rushed . . .

"Don't worry," said Little Bear.
"You're safe here." And he sat them
down to listen to the story. Everything
was all quiet and calm, when . . .

"We left our house and ran
and ran, 'til we got to your
door," squealed
the three pigs.

Little Bear let
them in and
locked the door.

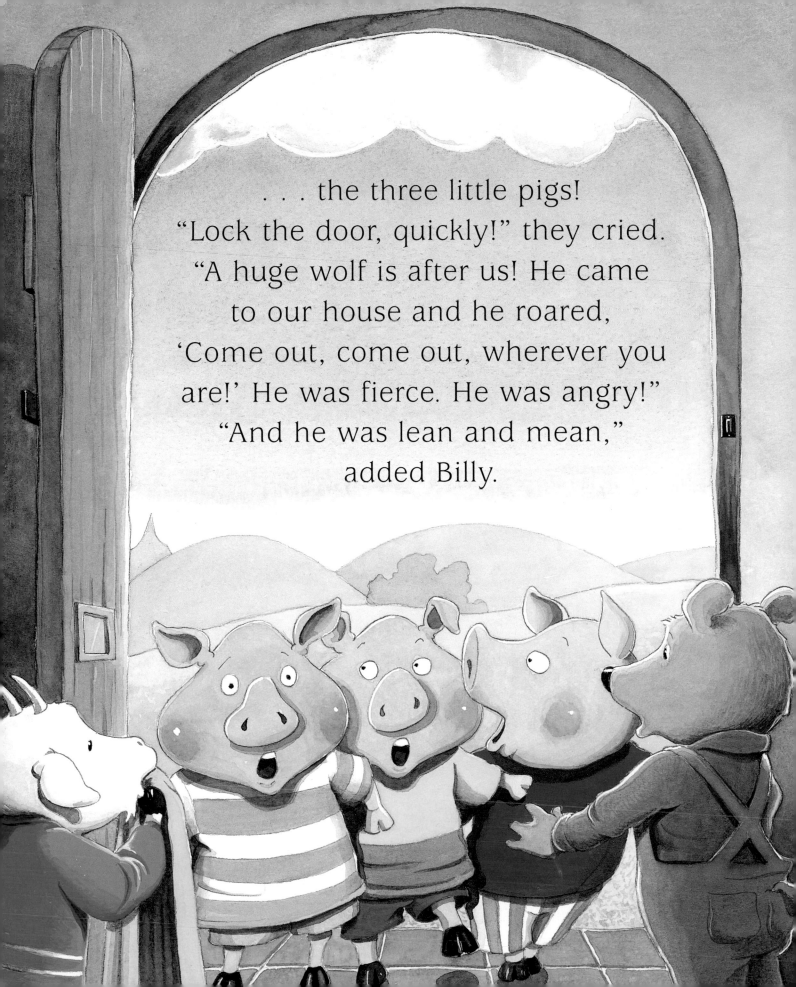

. . . the three little pigs!
"Lock the door, quickly!" they cried.
"A huge wolf is after us! He came
to our house and he roared,
'Come out, come out, wherever you
are!' He was fierce. He was angry!"
"And he was lean and mean,"
added Billy.

KNOCK KNOCK!
went the door!
"Who's there?" called Little Bear.
"It's the Squealer Boys!
Please let us in."

Little Bear lifted the
latch, opened
the door and in trotted . . .

Little Bear sat Billy down.
"Don't worry," he said. "You're safe here."
And he started to read Billy a story.
Everything was cozy and quiet, when . . .

"I saw him up on the mountain," the little goat whimpered. "I saw his long, black shadow. He looked lean and mean, so I ran and ran 'til I got to your door!"

. . . Little Billy Goat Gruff!
"Lock the door, quickly!" bleated
Billy. "A wolf is after me! And he
shouted, 'Come out, come out,
wherever you are!'"

"It's Billy," a tiny voice bleated. "Please let me in." Little Bear lifted the latch, opened the door and in trotted . . .

Knock! Knock! went the door. "Who's there?" asked Little Bear, jumping down from his chair.

One quiet afternoon, while Father Bear
was in the yard chopping wood, Little
Bear sat reading his favorite book.
All was cozy and peaceful, when,

For Rob O'Connor

ISBN 0-439-31453-4

12 11 10 9 8 7 6 5 4 3 2 1   01 02 03 04 05 06

Printed in China

First American Scholastic edition, December 2001

WOLF
at the DOOR!

Nick Ward

SCHOLASTIC INC.

New York Toronto London Auckland Sydney
Mexico City New Delhi Hong Kong Buenos Aires

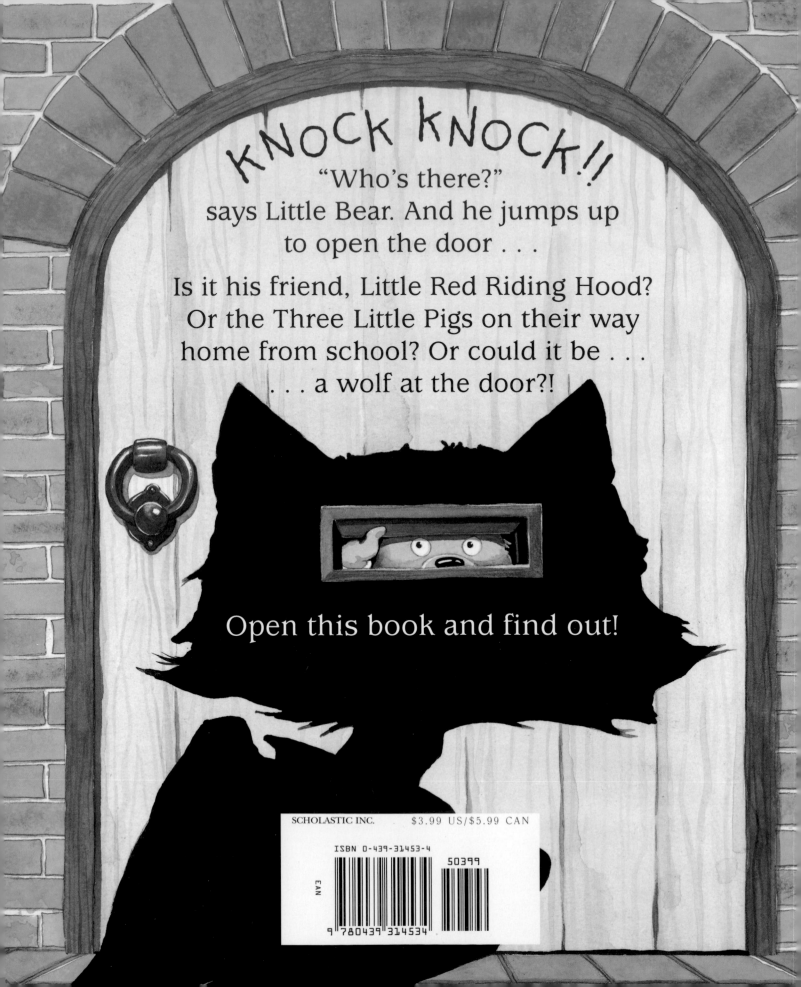

KNOCK KNOCK!!
"Who's there?"
says Little Bear. And he jumps up
to open the door . . .

Is it his friend, Little Red Riding Hood?
Or the Three Little Pigs on their way
home from school? Or could it be . . .
. . . a wolf at the door?!

Open this book and find out!

SCHOLASTIC INC. $3.99 US/$5.99 CAN

ISBN 0-439-31453-4

EAN

9 780439 314534   50399